Thank You

THANK YOU

Thank You

THANK YOU

You

THANK YOU

Thank You

Thank You

THANK YOU

Thank You

nk You

Thank You

THANK YOU

Thank You

THANK YOU

Thank You

Thank You

To the brightest lights
that are in my life,
Eliana and Weston.
Thank you, thank you, thank you
for being exactly who you are.

THIS BOOK IS GIVEN WITH LOVE

_____

_____

For all inquiries, please contact us at:
info@puppysmiles.org

To see more of our books, visit us at:
www.PuppyDogsAndIceCream.com

A Daily Gratitude Book
for Kids and Adults

Thank You
Thank You
Thank You

Written by Melissa Peck
Illustrated by Kendall Antosh

The two most important,
most powerful words,
you will ever speak
my little one are...

THANK YOU

There are so many things
to be thankful for
in this great, big world.

So many things, in fact,
we often take for granted and, instead,
we focus on what we lack.

This is a list of some little things
that are actually quite big.
Things we can be grateful for
and help us change the way we live.

Thank you

Thank you

Thank you

TREES

For your beauty
and the fresh air
you give

Thank you

Thank

Thank you

YOU

JOY

For showing me happiness
and how to live

Thank you
Thank you
Thank you
IMAGI

For keeping me playful, creative,
and giving space to be me

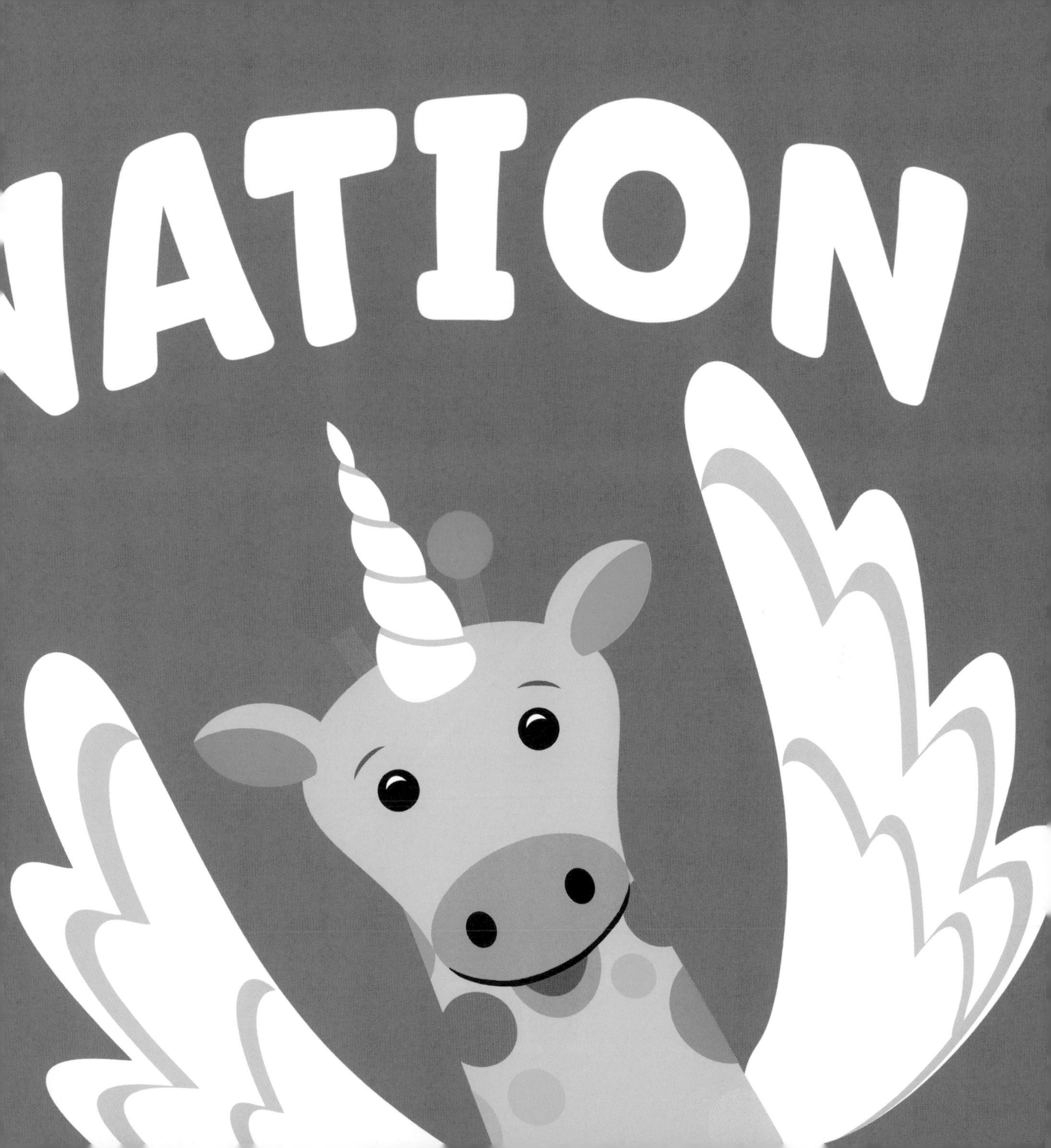
NATION

MOON AND STARS

For the magical light shows
you let everyone see

Thank you

Thank you

Thank you

HUGS

For showing support
and lifting me up
when I'm
feeling down

Thank you
Thank you
Thank you

FLOWERS

For your lovely smell and
spreading beauty all around

Thank you

Thank you

Thank you

OCEAN

For providing a home
where creatures can thrive

Thank you

Thank you

Thank you

MUSIC

For your peace
and your calm,

your wiggle
and your jive

you

Thank you

SADNESS

For showing what
strength and courage
are all about

Thank you
Thank you
Thank you

SUN

For the warmth you give,
both inside and out

Thank you

Thank you

Thank you

EVERY PERSON

For being you,
and for doing
your part

Thank you

Thank you

Thank you

BREATH

For filling me with life
in my beating heart

Thank you

Thank you

Thank you

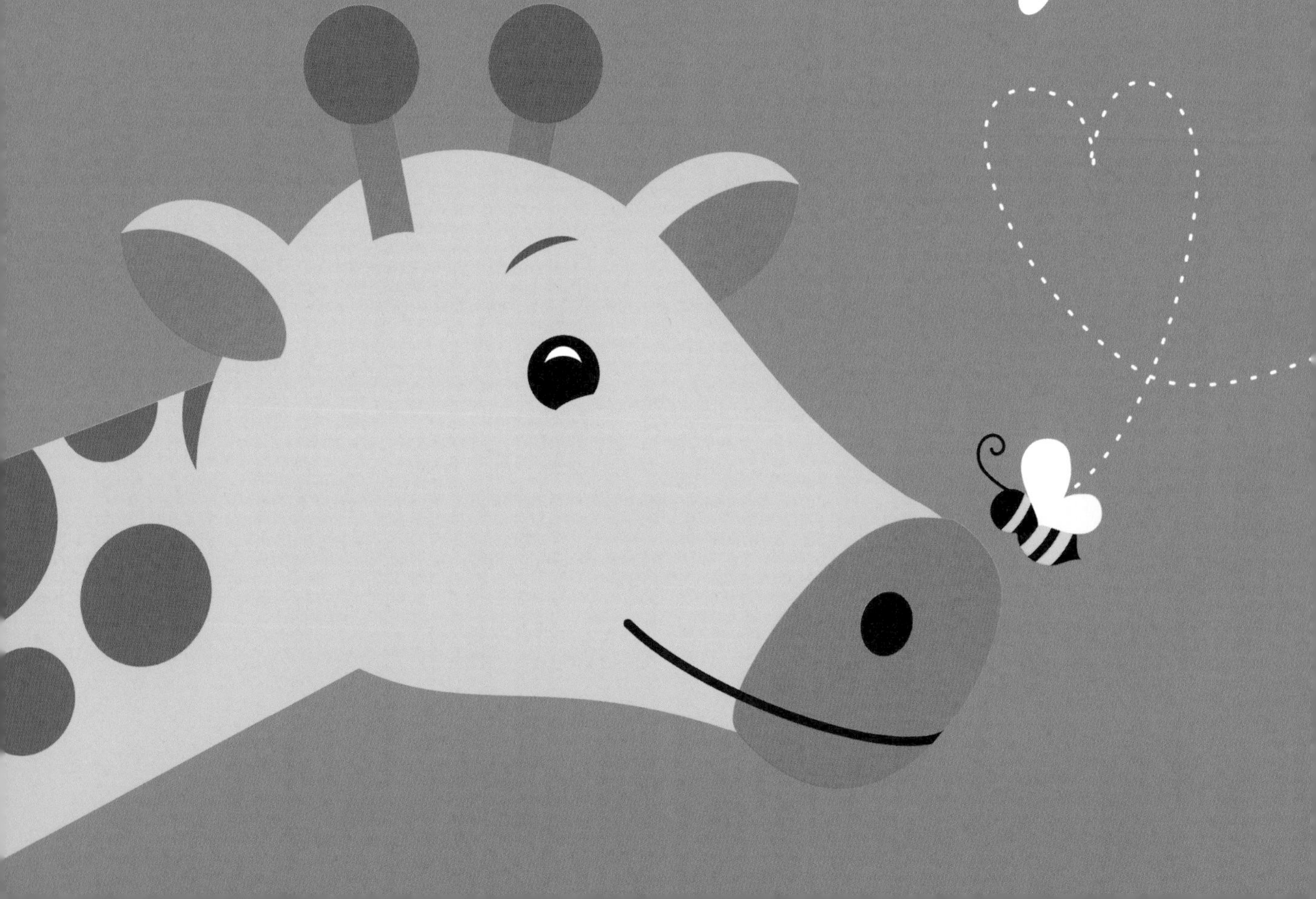

BEES

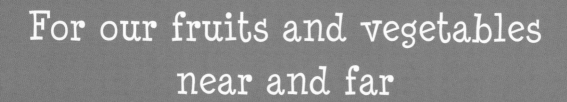

For our fruits and vegetables
near and far

Thank you

Thank you

Thank you

LOVE

For making us
who we are

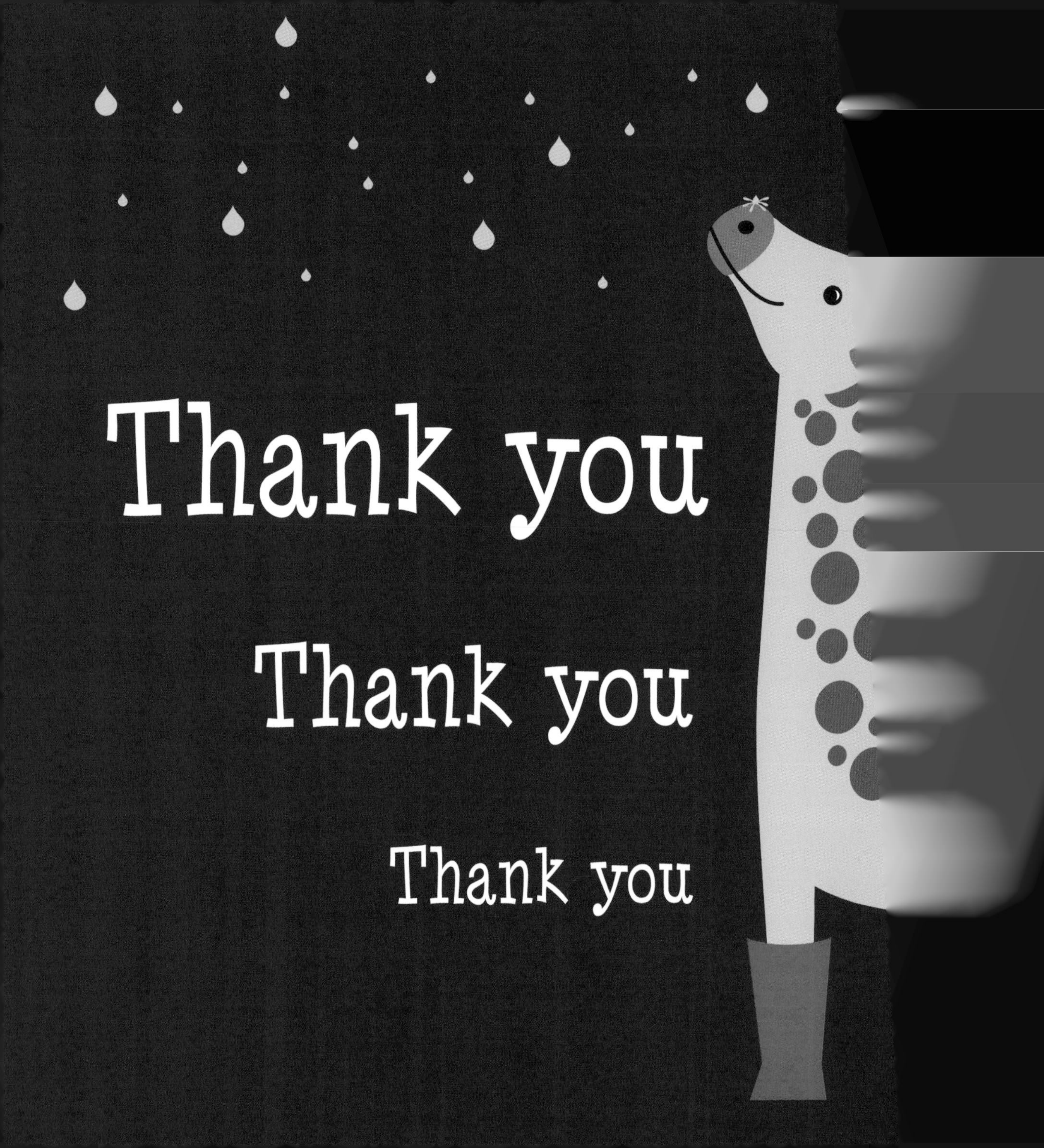
Thank you
Thank you
Thank you

RAIN

For helping all
living things grow

Thank you

Thank

COLORS

For painting the world
with a rainbow

you

Thank you

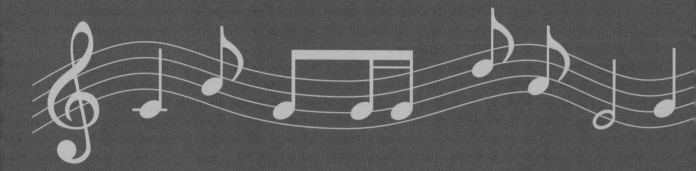

Thank you

Thank you

Thank you

BIRDS

For your sweet
and beautiful song

Thank you

Thank you

Thank you

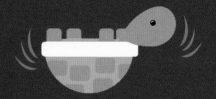

KINDNESS

For teaching me
right from wrong

Thank you
Thank you
Thank you

BED

For the safety and comfort
to dream the night away

Thank you

Thank you

Thank you

SLEEP

For resting my body
for another day

Thank you
Thank you
Thank you

ME

In this moment,
in this life,
in this body

It doesn't matter
how much or little you've got.
When you just look around
you can find quite a lot.

Whether you're feeling
happy or sad.
Whether you're having
a good day or bad.

There are ALWAYS things
you can be thankful for.
Now, little one...
can you think of more?

Thank you
Thank you
Thank you

Thank you

Write down **10** things you are thankful for:

1 _____

2 _____

3 _____

4 _____

5 _____

6 _____

7 _____

8 _____

9 _____

10 _____

Draw the things you are thankful for today!

Claim your FREE Gift!

🐾 Visit: 🐾
PDICBooks.com/Gift

Thank you for purchasing

Thank You, Thank You, Thank You

and welcome to the Puppy Dogs & Ice Cream family.

We're certain you're going to love the little gift

we've prepared for you at the website above.

THANK YOU

Thank You

Thank You

hank You

Thank You

Th

THANK YOU

THANK YOU

hank You

THANK YOU

Thank You

THANK YOU

T

Thank You

hank You

THANK YOU